Karen's adventure

It was the first day of the holidays. Karen had come to stay with her grandmother. 'I think I'm going to have an adventure today,' said Karen.

'Well, before you do, you'd better put on your wellington boots,' laughed Gran. 'It's been raining all night and the garden is very muddy. I'm going into the orchard to chop up some branches for the fire. If you need me that's where I'll be.'

1

Gran's house was in the country. It was old and
large and she had to work very hard to keep it neat
and tidy. 'This big old place is getting too much
for me to manage,' she would say to Karen.

The gardens were a mess. They were so big that
Gran couldn't look after them properly. 'Just look
at that grass,' Gran would sigh. 'I keep on cutting
it down but it keeps on coming back.' Most of the
gardens were overgrown with weeds and bushes.

Karen went down to the bottom of the vegetable garden. She was a long way from the house. There was a high wall around the garden and Karen wondered what was behind it. There was a wooden door in the wall but it was locked and chained. 'Nobody has used that door for years and years,' thought Karen. 'I wonder what is on the other side.'

'If I climb up that tree,' she thought, 'I shall be able to see over.' It wasn't easy but at last Karen reached the top. She found she could get from the tree on to the wall. Below her she saw an untidy little garden with a broken-down greenhouse in the middle of it. 'The only way in is through that old locked door,' she thought.

4

Karen noticed a wooden ladder leaning against the wall. 'If I walk along the top of the wall I'll be able to get down the ladder and explore the old greenhouse,' she thought.

It felt strange in the garden. Karen looked at the tall weeds and shivered. It was colder and darker on that side of the wall. Wasps and bluebottles buzzed around the greenhouse and flew in and out of the broken window panes.

Karen pushed open the broken door and went inside.
There were spiders' webs everywhere and green moss
was growing over the rotten window frames. There
was nothing in the greenhouse but a few broken
plant pots and a dusty old desk. 'What a strange
thing to find in a greenhouse,' thought Karen. In
the drawers she found some dead beetles and a
wooden box. It was black and shiny and it had red
signs on the lid.

Inside the box was a small green egg. 'This is very strange,' thought Karen. 'I'd better show it to Gran.'

It was difficult climbing back up the ladder while holding the box. Karen had to be very careful not to break the egg.

Gran was still in the orchard, chopping wood for
the fire. 'What have you found?' she asked.

'I'm not sure,' said Karen. 'It looks like an
egg. I found it in the old greenhouse.'

'Which old greenhouse?' asked Gran, looking
worried. Karen told her how she had climbed over
the wall and what she had found on the other side.

'Oh dear,' said Gran. 'I should have told you
not to go over the wall. The door in the wall was
locked up by my grandfather long before I was born.'

'I can't think why,' said Karen. 'There was just
a greenhouse and an old desk.'

Gran put on her glasses and looked at the box.
'The writing on the lid is Chinese,' she said.
'My grandfather used to live in China. He must
have brought this back with him.'

'Why did he lock up the garden?' asked Karen.

'Nobody knows,' replied Gran. 'When my sisters
and I were small we were never allowed to play in
that part of the garden, but that was a long time
ago. I don't suppose it matters any more.'

'I'll trace out this writing and send it to my
friend, Yin Ling,' said Karen. 'Her parents will be
able to tell us what it says.'

'I'll put the box on the dining room mantlepiece.
It will be safe there,' said Gran.

That night there was a terrible storm. The wind
howled around the house and shook the window frames.
The thunder crashed and lightning lit up the sky.

When Karen got up the next morning the first thing
she did was to go and look at the egg. Somehow
the box had fallen off the mantlepiece during
the night. Bits of shell lay all over the
fire-place. Karen heard a strange noise like
a mouse squeaking or a baby bird chirruping. It was
coming from the ashes in the fire-place. 'Perhaps
it's a bird,' she thought. 'It might have
fallen down the chimney.'

It wasn't a bird. It did look rather like one,
but it had no feathers and it had four legs. On its
head it had two tiny horns.

'You must be a baby dragon,' said Karen.
She put the box back on the mantlepiece, swept
up the broken egg shell and put it in the dustbin.
Then she found a shoe-box and lined it with straw.
She lifted the dragon from the fire-place and laid
it gently in the shoe-box.

Karen decided that she would keep the dragon a
secret.

'The best place to hide you is back in the old greenhouse,' said Karen. She went down the garden, and climbed over the wall again. She made the baby dragon comfortable under one of the shelves. 'I expect you're hungry. I wonder what you would like to eat,' said Karen.

In the next few days Karen gave the dragon all sorts of food. It ate everything she brought but it always seemed to be hungry.

The dragon grew very fast. It had been the size of
a baby bird when Karen found it, but now it was as
big as a small dog and as green as grass. 'You're
always hungry,' said Karen. The dragon seemed
to smile.

'I suppose I ought to tell Gran,' thought Karen.
'She must be wondering where all the food is
going.' In the end she decided to keep the secret
a little longer.

One morning there was a telephone call from
Yin Ling. 'This message doesn't make sense,'
she said.

'What does it say?' asked Karen.

'It says "He's afraid of mirrors. Don't feed
him chicken."'

'"He's afraid of mirrors. Don't feed him chicken,"'
said Karen. 'What can that mean?'

'Where did the writing come from?' asked Yin Ling.

'It was on the lid of an old box,' answered Karen.

It rained all afternoon. Gran wouldn't let Karen
go outside. 'You can't go out in this, dear, you'll
get soaked,' she said.
'I'll just have to give the dragon two breakfasts
tomorrow,' thought Karen.
That night there was another storm. The dragon came
out of the greenhouse and climbed over the wall. He
made his way towards the house and climbed through
the kitchen window. He was looking for something
to eat.

   In the fridge was a roast chicken. The dragon
opened the fridge door and took the chicken in his
jaws. With a single gulp he swallowed it whole.

Then something strange began to happen. The dragon
began to grow bigger, and bigger, and bigger.
His teeth became longer and sharper, and
his wings began to spread and flap. He changed
from a grass green colour to a fiery red.

Karen woke up suddenly. 'That's funny,' she
thought. 'It sounds as if there's someone
downstairs in the kitchen. I'd better go and see.'
She put on her dressing gown and slippers and went
down the stairs.

18

Karen listened at the kitchen door. Everything was quiet. She opened the door and switched on the light. 'Oh no!' gasped Karen. 'How did you get in here and what's happened to you? You look different.' The dragon began to growl. 'You bad dragon,' said Karen, 'go back to the greenhouse at once.' But the dragon took no notice. He slid off the table and began to crawl towards her.

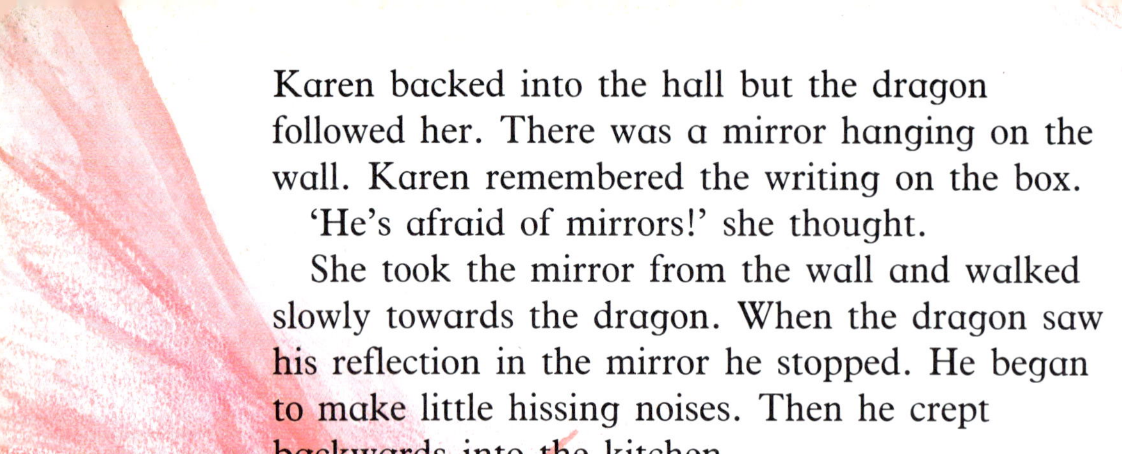

Karen backed into the hall but the dragon
followed her. There was a mirror hanging on the
wall. Karen remembered the writing on the box.
'He's afraid of mirrors!' she thought.
She took the mirror from the wall and walked
slowly towards the dragon. When the dragon saw
his reflection in the mirror he stopped. He began
to make little hissing noises. Then he crept
backwards into the kitchen.

Karen chased the dragon round the kitchen. He
jumped on to the table, gave a yelp, and flew
through the open window. Karen watched him fly up
into the stormy sky and away towards the full moon.
   'Well, I expect he's flown back to the land of
dragons, wherever that may be,' she thought.
'I wonder if I'll ever see him again.'

All about dragons

There are no such things as dragons but people
have been telling stories about them for thousands
of years. Do you know any stories about dragons?

In China dragons are supposed to make it rain. The
famous dragon dances were performed so that there
would be enough rain to make the crops grow.

There are dragon stories from all over the world.
Everybody has a different idea of what a dragon
looks like. What's your idea of a dragon?

A Chinese writer who lived over two thousand years
ago said a dragon was like this:

'His horns are like a stag's; he has a head like
a camel, eyes like a demon, a neck like a snake,
scales like a carp, claws like an eagle, and ears
like a cow.' (Wang Fu)

He doesn't mention wings!

On this page are some pictures of dragons. Can you find any more? Can you find any more descriptions of dragons?

Hott's First Dragon

Long, long ago, when monsters roamed the Earth,
the people of Denmark lived in fear of a terrible
dragon. It was so fierce and powerful that none of
the Danish King's warriors dared fight it. They
were not cowards, but they were not brave enough to
stand up to such a terrible monster.

Every night the dragon would come out of its den
and eat a flock of sheep or a herd of cattle.

In Norway lived a great hero called Bothva. The King of Denmark wrote to him, begging him to come and kill the dragon.

In those days it took many weeks to deliver a message. When Bothva read the King's letter, he set off at once to walk to Denmark.

When Bothva came to the King of Denmark's Hall there was nobody there to greet him. The King and all his people were out hunting. So he went into the Hall and looked around. He could hear a strange whimpering noise coming from behind a curtain.

Bothva gripped the hilt of his sword tightly, flung
back the curtain and found a young man hiding there.

'Help! Don't hurt me. Leave me alone you bully!'
cried the young man, in a trembling voice.

'Don't worry. I'm not going to hurt you,' laughed
Bothva. 'Tell me why you are so frightened.'

He had noticed that the young man was covered in
dirt and was shaking with fear. 'Come out, and find
me something to eat. How did you get so dirty?'

'It's because I get all the dirty jobs,' whimpered
Hott, for that was his name. 'I have to make the
fires, and cook the meals, and do the washing up,
and clean out the cowsheds. Everybody picks on me.'

'Why?' asked Bothva.

'Because I'm such a coward. Everybody tells me
I am. I'm scared of a mouse.'

'We'll see about that,' said Bothva. 'You could
be as brave as anyone if you wanted to be. We'll
make a start by getting you cleaned up.'

He made the young man go down to the stream and
scrub himself until he was as clean as a pebble.
When he was clean, Hott felt a bit better and
stopped crying.

The King was delighted to see Bothva. A great feast
was prepared to welcome him and Bothva sat at the
King's right hand. When the King described the
terrible dragon Bothva smiled. 'It doesn't sound
much of a dragon to me. I'm surprised you asked me
to come all the way from Norway when I'm sure that
even this boy here could deal with it!' He pointed
at Hott who nearly fainted with fright. Everybody
in the Hall roared with laughter at the idea of
poor little Hott killing the monster.

'I don't think you should make fun of him,' said
Bothva sternly. 'I can see that one day Hott will
be as brave as any of you.' He stood up and strode
out of the Hall, ordering Hott to follow him.

'Where are we going?' whimpered Hott.

'To kill the dragon and to make you brave,' said
Bothva, frowning at him. Now if Hott hadn't been
shaking with fear he would have run away but as
things were he had to follow Bothva.

They had gone only a few miles when they saw the
terrible monster coming towards them breathing
blue flames, and bellowing like a herd of bulls.

Hott was shaking with fear. Bothva watched as the beast came closer. 'Pull yourself together,' he ordered, 'it's only a dragon!' He drew his ice blue blade which glinted in the moonlight.
As the dragon sprang Bothva darted forward and plunged the sword deep into its heart. 'You see how it's done?' he said. 'It's easy when you know how.'

Hott couldn't believe his eyes. Then Bothva made him dip his finger in the dragon's blood. 'Taste it,' he said. 'There is magic in a dragon's blood.'

Hott put his finger in his mouth. He began to feel strange. He felt dizzy. Then he felt brave.

'I wish this dragon were alive again,' said Hott,
'I'd be quite happy to fight it myself.'

'That's given me an idea,' said Bothva. 'Help me prop this beast up so that it looks as if it's still alive and kicking. Then we'll go to see the King.'

Hott and Bothva strode into the Great Hall just as the King and his men were waking up.

'Come on,' said Bothva. 'Today we are going to look for that dragon. Follow me, everyone.'

The King and his men were terrified but they took their spears and swords and followed Bothva through the early morning mist.

Suddenly one of the men saw the dragon.

'Help! Bothva!' shouted the King. 'Do something before it has us for breakfast!'

'Sorry,' said Bothva, 'I never bully things that are weaker than myself. This looks like a job for a boy, not a man. Do you want to have a go Hott? I'll lend you my sword.'

'Certainly,' said Hott. 'If nobody else wants to, I'll have a try.' He took Bothva's sword, walked calmly up to the monster, and chopped off its head.

Nobody bullied Hott again. The dragon's blood had made him the bravest man in Denmark. The King made him his champion and gave him chests full of bright yellow gold. Hott killed many dragons in his lifetime but nobody ever learned the secret of how he killed his first one.

The End